Stay, Little Seed

CRISTIANA VALENTINI · PHILIP GIORDANO

GREYSTONE KIDS

GREYSTONE BOOKS • VANCOUVER / BERKELEY

On the top of a hill, above a beautiful meadow,
lived a tree covered in seeds.
The seeds were small and silent,
but one day they would be big trees of their own,
reaching for the sky and whispering with the wind.
They couldn't wait.

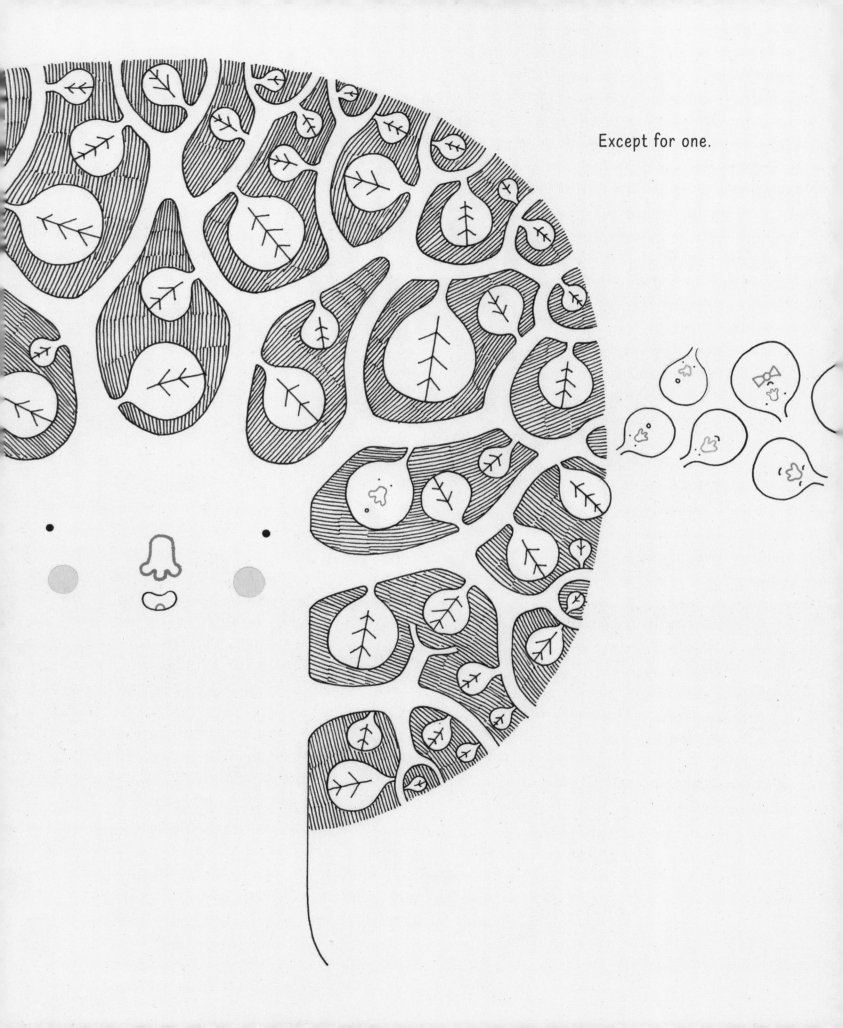

Except for one.

When a great wind came and blew the seeds
north and south and even Who Knows Where,
one tiny seed stayed.

It clung to its branch in the tree.

"Oh," said the tree. "You're still here?
Hurry up, or you'll be left behind.
Don't you want to join all your brothers and sisters?"

But the tiny seed didn't move.
Except to shake its head, no.

The tiny seed was the only one

that had ever tried to stay.

The tree knew it needed

to let go of its branch,

and fly off to Who Knows Where,

if it was going to grow big and strong.

But the tree had a tender heart.

It didn't know anything about Who Knows Where.

Would the tiny, cautious seed be welcome there?

Besides, sometimes the tree found it lonely on the hill.

Maybe the seed could stay after all.

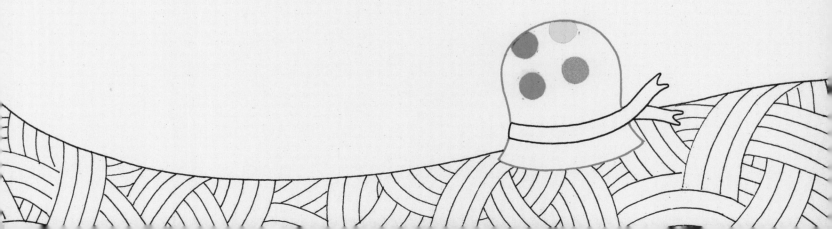

The next day, the tree was
planning to encourage the seed to leave.
But then it saw rain clouds coming.
It wasn't fun to travel in the rain.

So instead, the tree protected the tiny seed
from the big, wet drops.

"Just one more day," said the tree.

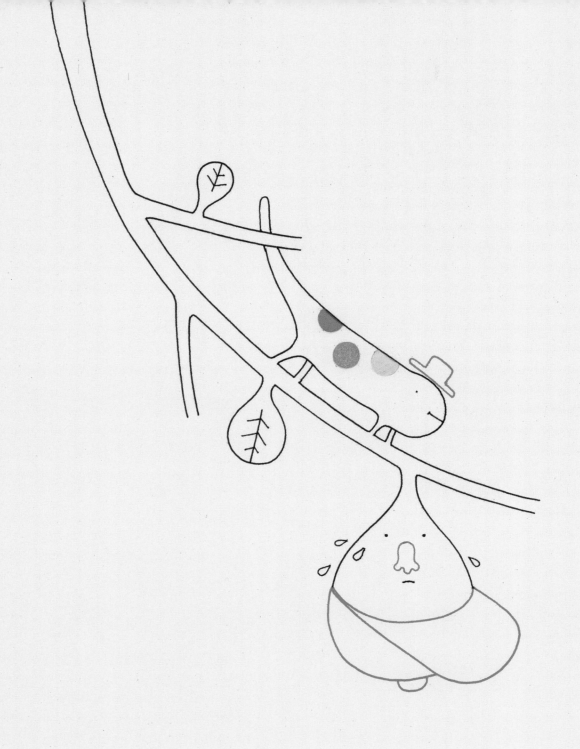

But it rained for a WHOLE week.

And when at last the sun shone,
the tree saw a new problem.
It would be terrible if the seed got a sunburn.

"You can't go out in the sun without a hat, can you?"
The seed, who could only imagine a hat,
supposed the tree must be right.

"Just one more day," said the tree.

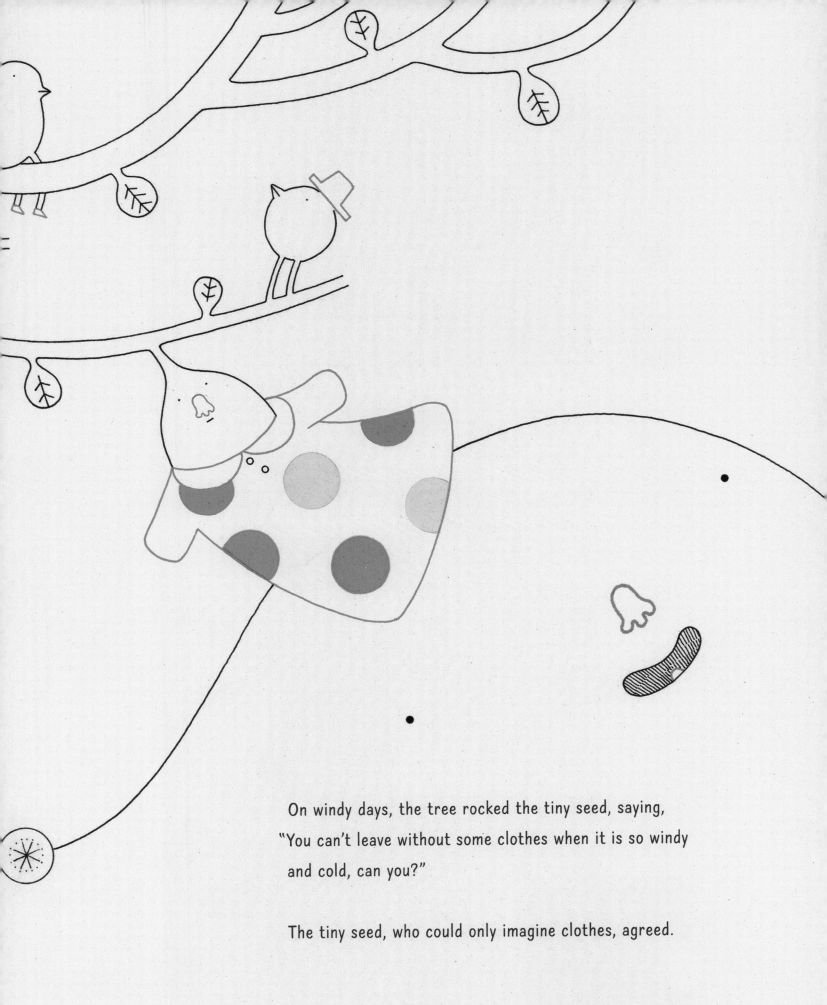

On windy days, the tree rocked the tiny seed, saying,
"You can't leave without some clothes when it is so windy
and cold, can you?"

The tiny seed, who could only imagine clothes, agreed.

And so it went.

"You can't go anywhere without boots, can you?" said the tree.

"No, I can't," agreed the seed.

Just one more day . . .

just one more day . . .

just one more day!

The tiny seed didn't leave.
The tree kept it close, watching over it,
worrying over what would happen
if it went off to Who Knows Where.

The tree and the seed were both afraid of that.

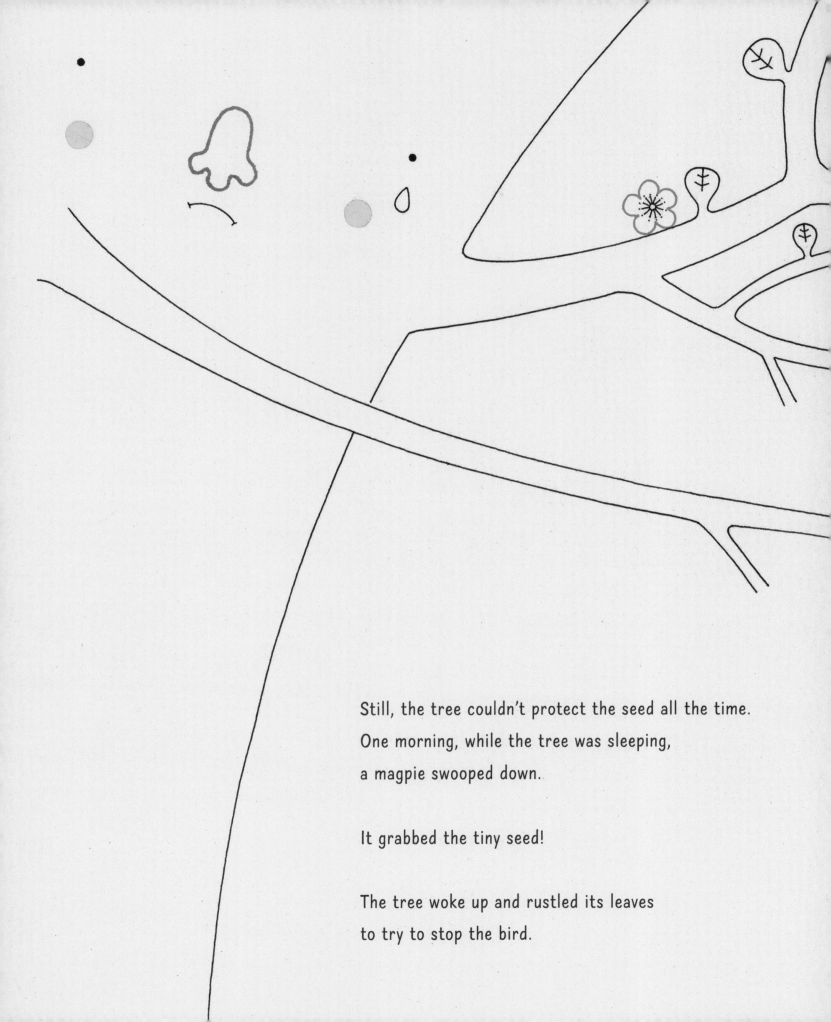

Still, the tree couldn't protect the seed all the time.
One morning, while the tree was sleeping,
a magpie swooped down.

It grabbed the tiny seed!

The tree woke up and rustled its leaves
to try to stop the bird.

It was too late.
The magpie had already
broken the seed off its branch.

But then the bird opened its mouth to laugh,
and the seed fell

down,

down,

down,

all the way to Who Knows Where.

"Oh no! Is my tiny seed okay?" worried the tree.
The tree worried and wondered for a long time.

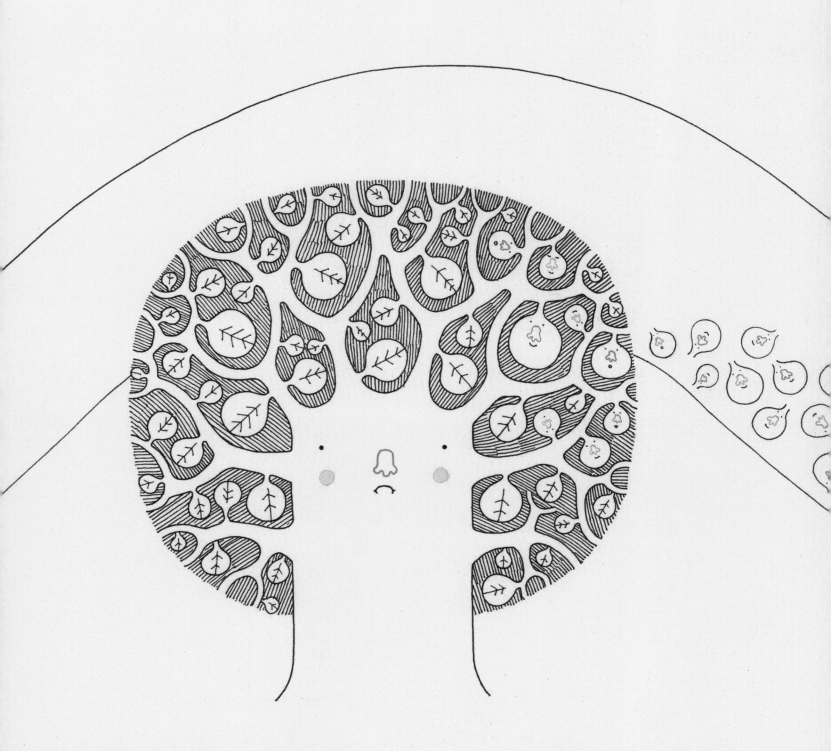

As the seasons passed
and other seeds came and left,
the tree never stopped wondering with its tender heart.
Until, one warm day, the tree heard a voice
drift up from below. "Hello? Hello?"

In the wind, the tree's tip-top branches leaned over.

It recognized its seed at once—only now it wasn't
a tiny seed at all, but a sapling, beautiful and strong.

"Oh, my dear, tiny seed!" the tree called back. "Hello! Hello!"

Who Knows Where wasn't so far away. It was the
beautiful meadow, just below the hill. And the tiny seed
hadn't needed a hat or clothes or boots after all.

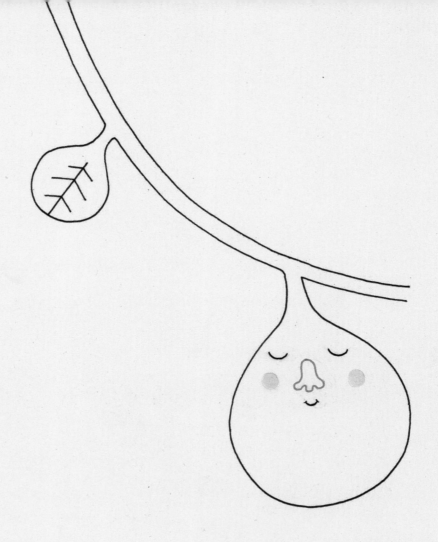

It had made a safe journey, all by itself.

To my gifts: Anna, Erika, Fiorenza, Marisa,
Nicoletta, Maura, Arianna, Erika, and Stella. — C.V.

To all those travelling east
and to those whose journey has yet to begin. — P.G.

Originally published in Italy in 2008 as *Chissadove*
Text and illustrations copyright © 2020 ZOOlibri—Reggio Emilia—Italia
First published in English by Greystone Books in 2020

20 21 22 23 24   5 4 3 2 1

Greystone Kids / Greystone Books Ltd.
greystonebooks.com

Cataloguing data available from Library and Archives Canada
ISBN 978-1-77164-646-8 (cloth)
ISBN 978-1-77164-647-5 (epub)

Editing by Kallie George
Copy editing by Antonia Banyard
Proofreading by DoEun Kwon
English text design by Sara Gillingham Studio
Cover illustration by Philip Giordano

Printed and bound in Malaysia on ancient-forest-friendly paper by Tien Wah Press

Greystone Books gratefully acknowledges the Musqueam, Squamish, and Tsleil-Waututh peoples
on whose land our office is located.

Greystone Books thanks the Canada Council for the Arts, the British Columbia Arts Council,
the Province of British Columbia through the Book Publishing Tax Credit, and the Government of Canada
for supporting our publishing activities.

   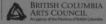